PUFFIN BOOKS

Addy the Baddy

Margaret Joy was born on Tyneside, and has lived in various parts of the British Isles. She worked for some years as a teacher, while writing children's stories for radio and television, then in book form. Recently she has hung up her chalk, in order to make the most of life with her retired husband, their four grown-up children, their grandchildren, and their neurotic cat. Now settled in North Wales, she enjoys living and writing in beautiful surroundings.

By the same author

Addy the Baddy

Margaret Joy

Illustrated by
Lauren Child

PUFFIN BOOKS

PUFFIN BOOKS

Published by the Penguin Group
Penguin Books Ltd, 27 Wrights Lane, London W8 5TZ, England
Penguin Books USA Inc., 375 Hudson Street, New York, New York 10014, USA
Penguin Books Australia Ltd, Ringwood, Victoria, Australia
Penguin Books Canada Ltd, 10 Alcorn Avenue, Toronto, Ontario, Canada M4V 3B2
Penguin Books (NZ) Ltd, 182–190 Wairau Road, Auckland 10, New Zealand

Penguin Books Ltd, Registered Offices: Harmondsworth, Middlesex, England

First published by Viking 1993
Published in Puffin Books 1995
1 3 5 7 9 10 8 6 4 2

Text Copyright © Margaret Joy, 1993
Illustrations copyright © Lauren Child, 1993
All rights reserved

The moral right of the author has been asserted

Filmset in Linotron Times New Roman

Printed in England by Clays Ltd, St Ives plc

1.

Addy sat looking at the toast on her plate.

"I don't want any toast. I don't want any breakfast at all," she said.

"You'll be hungry at school," warned her mum.

"I don't want to go to school," said Addy.

"But it's a new school –
you'll like it," said her mum.

"I don't want to go to a new
school and I won't like it," said
Addy. "I want to go back to
my old school."

"But you can't – we've
moved," said her mum. "You'll
soon get to like the new school.
You'll soon make new friends."

Addy scowled and bit into
the toast. "I don't want any
new friends," she said.
"Friends are silly."

"I'll make your favourite
pancakes for tea," promised
her mum. "Now sit still while I
brush your hair."

She brushed Addy's hair and put bobbles on her plaits. Then she looked her up and down: "Very smart," she said. "That blue and grey uniform is lovely. And I like the way your tie is fixed on elastic so you only have to stretch it over your head. That seems very sensible."

Addy didn't say anything.

"Now," said her mum cheerfully, "put this clean hanky in your pocket, then get your coat on and we'll be ready."

Ten minutes later they set off along the road to the new school. Addy held on tightly to her mum's hand. She was still scowling and she kept muttering: "Silly school, silly new school, silly new friends."

"What's that you're saying?" asked her mum.

"Didn't say anything," muttered Addy.

"Oh, I thought I heard you say something," said her mum.

"It was just my tongue wobbling about in my mouth," said Addy, "Like this!" She showed her mum.

"Ah, I see," said her mum.

Addy suddenly stopped walking.

"I can hear something," she said, "What's that noise?"

They stood still and listened. It sounded like a flock of birds screeching in the next street but it was really the sound of shouting and laughing.

"It's coming from your new school," said Addy's mum. "It's the children in the playground."

Addy scowled again. "Silly
children. Silly playground.
Silly school," she said aloud.
But to herself she added: "And
anyway, I shan't be staying
there long. I'll see that I
don't . . ."

Addy and her mum went first
to the head teacher's room.

"Hallo," said the
head teacher, "I'm Mrs
Bradley."

"This is Adelaide," said
Addy's mum. "But she's called
Addy."

Mrs Bradley shook Addy's hand, then her mum's. Addy looked round while they talked.

There was a fish tank against one wall. Bubbles popped on

the top of the water. The fish
stared at Addy. She stared
back. On the wall were photos
of lots of children smiling.
Addy scowled at them.

"I'll come and fetch you at home time," said her mum. "Then we'll have those pancakes."

She gave Addy a big hug and a kiss. Then she went off to buy lemons for the pancakes.

2.

Mrs Bradley took Addy's
hand. They walked across the
hall, where some children were
dancing about. They were
being angry giants and making
horrid faces. Addy made
horrid faces back at them. Mrs
Bradley opened a door.

"Here's your classroom,"
she said. "And this is your

teacher, Miss Mackie. Miss
Mackie, this is Addy. She's
come to live near here, so she's
had to leave her old school."

"Hallo, Addy," said Miss
Mackie. "I'm sure you'll soon
get used to us."

Miss Mackie had a nice face
and curly black hair. She
showed Addy where to hang
her coat and where the toilets
were. Then she said: "Come
and sit over here with Kath.
You'll look after Addy, won't
you, Kath?"

Kath nodded, staring at
Addy.

"Don't want to be looked after," said Addy, scowling.

"You won't know what to do," said Kath.

"I don't care," said Addy, "I'm not staying here long."

"Oh," said Kath. She stared at Addy's face and then at her little plaits. Kath shook her pony-tail and said proudly: "My hair's long enough to sit on."

"That's nothing," said Addy, "I can touch my nose with my tongue." She showed Kath how she did it. Kath tried, but her tongue wouldn't reach that far.

"That's nothing," said Kath.
"I've got a black nail. It got
squashed in the door." She
showed Addy the black nail.

"Yuk," said Addy. "But
that's nothing – my Uncle
Tom's only got three fingers on
one hand."

22

Kath stared, then she showed Addy her number book. "I'm doing tens and units," she said.

"I can do them," said Addy.

"Taking away," said Kath.

"Easy," declared Addy.

"And carrying," said Kath.

"Easy peasy," boasted
Addy.

Kath bent over her book and
then began to count on her
fingers. Addy sat and touched
her nose with her tongue. She
took no notice of the paper and
crayons Miss Mackie had given

her. After a while she got up and went to the toilet. She shut the door and sat there.

"I can't do tens and units, taking away and carrying," she thought. "What shall I do?"

Two big tears began to roll down her cheeks. She brushed them away. "Silly sums!" she thought. 'Silly, *silly* sums – and silly school. I'm not stopping here long anyway."

Then she thought: "If I'm bad, really really bad, perhaps they'll make Mum come and take me home straight away . . ." She began to think of what she could do . . .

She opened the toilet door and walked over to the wash-basin. She made her hands all soapy, then she wrote on the mirror with a soapy finger:

SILLY SUMS

Underneath that, she wrote:

ADDY THE BADDY

She dried her hands on a paper towel, screwed it up into a ball, and stuck it in the plug-hole. Then she turned on the tap and went back to her classroom.

"Would you like to draw me
a picture?" asked Miss Mackie.

Addy began to draw a
house. She coloured the door
blue. She pressed very hard on
the blue crayon to make it
bright. Snap! The crayon broke

inside its paper. Addy looked at the other crayons. She picked them up one by one and pressed them very hard on the table. Snap! Snap! Snap! They were all breaking inside their paper wrappers.

"You're breaking them," said Kath. "They're new crayons. I'm telling."

"No, you're not," said Addy. "I'll pull your hair."

"No you won't," said Kath. "I'll tell Miss Mackie."

But Miss Mackie was rushing over to the toilets where she could hear water running. She opened the door and discovered a wash-basin overflowing. A huge pool of water was slowly spreading across the floor.

"Help!" exclaimed Miss Mackie.

She turned off the tap and pulled the ball of paper out of

the plug-hole. Then she grabbed a mop and began to push the water away down the corridor.

The bell rang. It was playtime.

"Out you go," said Miss Mackie. "And KEEP OUT OF THE WATER!"

Kath tried to tell her about Addy, but Miss Mackie wasn't listening.

"That was *quite* bad," thought Addy, pleased. "For a start, anyway. If I go on like this, they'll send for Mum and make her take me away . . ."

3.

Everyone put their coats on and went out into the playground. Bobby was just behind Addy. He looked at her little plaits. They were hanging over her shoulders like little ropes. He gave them both a hard tug.

"Don't you dare do that!" shouted Addy.

Bobby stepped back and looked at her.

"If you do that again, I'll . . . spit," said Addy.

"Girls can't spit."

"Yes, they can."

"Go on then, I dare you."

Addy rolled her mouth
together and spat across the
playground.

"OOh-er."

The others looked at her
admiringly.

"You can't do that," said
Paula.

"Yes, I can – I've just done it," said Addy.

"I'm telling," said Kath.

"Go on then," said Addy, "I dare you."

"Huh," said Kath. "Who do you think you are?"

"I'm Addy the Baddy," said Addy. "And I'm not stopping here long – my mum will come and take me away."

She put her hands in her pockets and scowled at them all. Then she felt something with her fingers. Her mum had put a surprise in her pocket. Addy pulled it out. It was a paper bag – with something inside.

"Look what I've got," she
said.

"Oooh, liquorice" said Kath.

"Want a bit?" asked Addy,
pulling a piece off one of the
bootlaces.

Kath took some, so did Jane and Paula, who were with them. Then Addy remembered that she was going to be bad. She looked round. What could she do? Suddenly she had an idea – She would frighten that Bobby and those other horrible boys.

She pushed one bit of liquorice up under her top lip on one side of her mouth, then a second bit on the other side. They looked just like black fangs. She waved her arms up and down and flapped her coat. Then she ran at some of the boys.

"Whoooo-oooo-whaaaaaaah!" she screeched.

"Look at those fangs," said Kevin.

"Hey, it's Dracula," laughed Ray.

"That's great!" shouted Bobby.

Kath and Jane and Paula looked at one another. Then they too stuck their liquorice under their top lips at each side of their mouths. They began to flap their coats and screech in loud voices. "Whooooo-ooooo-whaaaaah!"

Now they looked like Dracula too.

"That's a great game," said
Bobby. "Can we play?"

Addy gave the boys some
liquorice each. Soon there was
a Dracula Gang screeching
and flapping its way round the
playground.

41

"Whoooo-wooooo-
whaaaaaah!" they yelled.

When the bell went, they
pulled their fangs out and ate
them. Their mouths looked
rather black.

"That was great," said Kath,
chewing.

"Yes," said Addy. "It was
ace!"

Then she remembered that
she was Addy the Baddy – and
she tried to stop smiling.

4.

Some of the class were making dinosaurs with plasticine. Miss Mackie said to them: "Later on, you can paint a huge diplodocus and we'll hang it on the wall behind your plasticine models. But just for now, see if you can work on your own, because Addy and I are going to do some number work."

Miss Mackie came to sit next to Addy and they talked about the sort of things she had done in her old school. Then they tried some sums together.

"Very good," said Miss Mackie, watching Addy working, "You're getting on like a house on fire. You've nothing to worry about there, Addy."

Addy worked out a few more sums. She got all of them right first time.

"Well done," said Miss Mackie. "Now I think it's your turn to do some painting, Addy."

Addy was pleased – until she remembered that she was going to be bad. What could she do next? She began to think.

She put on an apron and
went over to the pots of paint.
She took the brush out of the
pink pot, plopped it into the
green paint and stirred it
round.

Then she took the brush out
of the black paint, dipped it
into the yellow and stirred it
round.

She took the brush out of the

blue paint and stirred it into
the brown. Then she took all of
the brushes, dipped them into
each other's pots and stirred
and stirred. It was great fun!

Soon the paint in all the pots
was a sort of greeny-brown
colour. Addy waited for Miss
Mackie to come and see.

"Oh!" said Miss Mackie.
"You've mixed up all the
colours, Addy."

She sounded very surprised. Addy waited for Miss Mackie to be cross. But all she said was: "You've made just the colour we needed for the diplodocus, Addy – what a stroke of luck. Now we've got eight pots full of diplodocus colour. You can start work on it straight away."

Addy was very surprised. But she painted for ages and really enjoyed it. When the diplodocus was more than half painted, Miss Mackie said: "That's good."

Addy was pleased. Then she remembered that she was

Addy the Baddy. She had to stop feeling pleased. She put on a scowl instead.

"Time to go into the hall," said Miss Mackie.

"Ah, great," said everyone.

Addy watched the others, then copied what they were doing. They changed into their PE clothes and stood ready with bare feet. Everyone was shivering – perhaps because they were cold, perhaps because they were excited.

"It's great on the apparatus," said Kath. "There's a box and bars and balancing."

Addy didn't say anything, but she stopped scowling. Now she was excited too. She knew all about apparatus work. She had always enjoyed it in her old school.

She loved holding out her arms to balance on the bar, like a clown on a tight rope. She loved swinging from hand to hand, like a monkey swinging from branch to branch. She loved doing forward rolls, tucked into a little ball like a hedgehog.

The children went into the hall, still shivering.

"OK, we'll have some

jigging and jogging to warm
you up, first," said Miss
Mackie.

She played some pop music
and they began to dance to it.
Soon they felt quite loosened
up and much warmer. After
that she divided them into
groups.

"You can be in the same
group as Kath," said Miss
Mackie to Addy. "She'll show
you what to do."

Addy remembered that she
was Addy the Baddy. She
would give them all a shock.

"I know what to do," she said.

She ran to the rope hanging from the ceiling. She caught hold of it with both hands and pulled herself up. She let the end of it twist round her legs. She pulled herself up and the rope slid down between her knees. She climbed up and up and up – until she reached the ceiling. Then she stayed there, like a sailor at the top of the mast. Everyone down below was looking up at her. They were quite amazed. They'd never seen anyone shin up the rope like that before. They all

burst out clapping. What a climber!

"Well done, Addy!" said Miss Mackie.

Addy blinked with surprise. She had climbed ropes hundreds of times in her old school, but no one had ever clapped her before. She slid down slowly, so that she didn't blister her hands.

After that, she enjoyed every minute of her time on the apparatus. But at last they had to stop. Miss Mackie said: "Back to class now."

"Aw," said everyone – Addy too.

5.

By dinner time Addy was really hungry. She thought about being bad and refusing to eat any dinner. Her tummy felt a bit funny this morning. But she was so hungry, she ate every scrap – except the sprouts. There were five small Brussels sprouts on her plate and Addy just couldn't manage them. Somehow just looking at them seemed to make her tummy feel more mixed up.

She looked round. All the other children were clearing their plates. They didn't seem to be having difficulty eating their sprouts. The dinner lady was on the other side of the room. Addy pulled her hanky out of her pocket and laid it flat on her lap. Then, quick as a flash, she swept the five small sprouts off the edge of the plate and on to the hanky. She bundled the whole lot back into her pocket. No one had noticed a thing.

There was banana jelly after that, and her tummy seemed to like it. Addy managed to finish it all.

"Good girl," said the dinner lady.

Addy didn't say anything.
She could feel the sprouts bulge
in the hanky in her pocket.

"I'm going out – coming?"
asked Kath.

They went into the
playground. The boys were
racing round, hiding behind
corners and firing at one
another. It looked a good
game.

"Can I play?" said Addy.

"No," said Bobby. "It's cowboys and Indians."

"Well, I'm an Indian," said Addy.

She pulled her tie off and

stretched the elastic round her forehead, so that the tie hung down at the back.

"I'm a squaw," she declared. "A baddy squaw."

"Yes, yes," shouted Kath. "So'm I."

She stretched her elastic tie round her forehead too. It hung down at the back over her long hair: "I'm a baddy squaw too!"

They raced round the playground, slapping their pretend ponies to make them gallop faster. The boys watched: "All right then," shouted Bobby. "You can play."

After that they all had a really good noisy game. The dinner lady was watching them. She said: "Sometimes cowboys have scarves over their mouths – to keep out the dust when they're galloping."

"Yes," said Kevin, "And bandits do too."

"Yes, bandits," said Ray. "I'll be a bandit – anyone got a hanky?"

"I have," said Addy.

She reached into her pocket and pulled out her hanky. Then she remembered – but it was too late. Five small sprouts flew out and shot across the playground.

"Oooh!" said Kevin.

"Sprouts," said Bobby.

"I'm telling," said Kath.

Addy burst into tears. She had stopped being a Baddy;

she just felt miserable.

"Oh, dear," said the dinner lady. She looked at Addy's hanky. There were green bits on it: "That's a bit sprouty," she said.

She pulled a pink handkerchief out of her own pocket and gave it to Addy, who wiped her eyes. The dinner lady clapped her hands at the other cowboys and Indians and shooed them away.

"Now," she said to Addy. "What's your name?"

"Addy," said Addy.

"Addy?" asked the dinner lady. "Is that short for something?"

"Adelaide," said Addy.

"Adelaide!" said the dinner lady. "What a beautiful name. You're the first Adelaide this

school has ever had."

"I'm not stopping at this school," said Addy, sniffing. "I'm being bad and my mummy will come and take me away."

"Oh," said the dinner lady. She sounded quite disappointed.

"Yes," said Addy, "I'm Addy the Baddy."

"Oh, I see," said the dinner lady. She took hold of Addy's hand. "Let's go and look for the sprouts and throw them away," she said.

"And while we do that I'll tell you a secret – I happen to know that tomorrow's dinner is roast chicken, baked potatoes and stuffing, with butterscotch ice-cream for afters . . ."

Just then the bell went. Addy saw Kath and ran in with her. She turned round and saw the dinner lady waving goodbye, so she waved back . . .

The afternoon passed quickly.

Addy and Kath played with the dressing-up clothes. Addy put on the witch's outfit.

At three o'clock, Addy's mum was waiting for her just outside the school door.

"Hallo, Addy," she said.

"Hallo, Mum," said Addy.

"I've got the lemons," said her mum.

"Lemons?" said Addy.

"Yes, for the pancakes," said her mum.

"Oh, them," said Addy. She took a deep breath. "Look, I've got a new book to read and a bookmark I made myself. I decorated it with felt tips, and I painted most of a dinosaur, and I ate all my dinner – "

"All of it?"

'Well, nearly all of it," said Addy, remembering the five small Brussels sprouts. "And I climbed to the top of the rope in the hall and they gave me a clap, and we played Dracula, and cowboys and Indians, and there was dressing-up and they said I was the horriblest witch they'd ever seen, and tomorrow for dinner we're going to have roast chicken and baked potatoes and carrots, then butterscotch ice-cream – "

"Bye, Addy," called Kath.

"Who's that?" whispered Kath's mum.

"Addy the Baddy," Kath whispered back.

"Bye, Kath," called Addy.

"That's Kath," said Addy. "She can sit on her hair and she's got a black nail that was squashed in the door. She's my new friend."

She pulled at her mother's hand. "Come on, let's go home. I can't wait for those pancakes, I'm starving. I bet I could eat six, or ten – or even fifty thousand. School makes you dead hungry, doesn't it?"